Julia Killingback wishes to acknowledge the
help and support of the Avon Fire Brigade
who supplied the Fire Prevention
and Safety Information in this book.

Busy Bears at the Fire Station

Julia Killingback

Methuen Children's Books

'Eat up your breakfast,' says Mr Bear.
'I have a surprise that we can share . . .

'Most days you stay at home to play
But you can come to work today!'
Who's coming?

'Welcome to the Fire Beargade!' says Chief Bear.
'When you need help we're *always* here!'

'Firefighter Busy Bear will show you round –
And don't forget, the alarm might sound!'
Do *you* think it will?

First, let's see what Firebears wear!
Who wants to try this yellow pair?

Each firebear has his own smart set
To keep him safe from heat and wet.
Who tried on Dad's jacket?

'Hold tight, Bears!' Each Firebear knows
How hard it is to hold that hose!

'So please remember, just take care.
Don't play with fire!' says Firefighter Bear.
You will take care, won't you?

Which sport would you like to do?
Join in our fun and get fit too!

'We have to be fit,' puffs Firefighter Bear,
'So we're ready to work just anywhere.'
BBBBBBBBB-RING!

Whizz down the pole, no time for stairs!
Jump into the engine, Firefighter Bears!
BLEE BLAH, BLEE BLAH, BLEE BLAH . . .

Thanks to the Firefighters help is on its way.
'Soon all will be well,' the Firefighters say.
Firefighters are *always* ready to help.

'Hello, we're back!' the Firebears shout.
'It didn't take long to put the fire out!'

'Are you hungry? Let's all eat.
Bears, please share our special treat.'
Would *you* like some too?

'Before we go home, we can climb up here.
Make the siren go!' shouts Baby Bear.
BLEE BLAH, BLEE BLAH, BLEE BLAH.

'Thank you for coming to see what we do.
REMEMBER YOUR FIRE BRIGADE CARES ABOUT YOU!
Goodbye!

SUPPORT YOUR
LOCAL FIRE
BEARGADE!

BOOKS ARE
GGGR-EAT!

First published in Great Britain in 1988
by Methuen Children's Books Ltd, 11 New Fetter Lane, London EC4P 4EE
Copyright © 1988 Julia Killingback
Printed in Hong Kong by
Wing King Tong Co Ltd
ISBN 0 416 06312 8